The Great
Thanksgiving Escape

To my family and those get-togethers
that unraveled beautifully.

ISBN 978-0-545-91283-9

Copyright © 2014 by Mark Fearing. All rights reserved. Published by Scholastic Inc., 557 Broadway, New York, NY 10012, by arrangement with Candlewick Press. SCHOLASTIC and associated logos are trademarks and/or registered trademarks of Scholastic Inc.

12 11 10 9 8 7 6 5 4 3 2 1   15 16 17 18 19 20/0

Printed in the U.S.A.

First Scholastic printing, October 2015

This book was typeset in Adobe Garamond.
The illustrations were done in pencil and completed digitally.

40

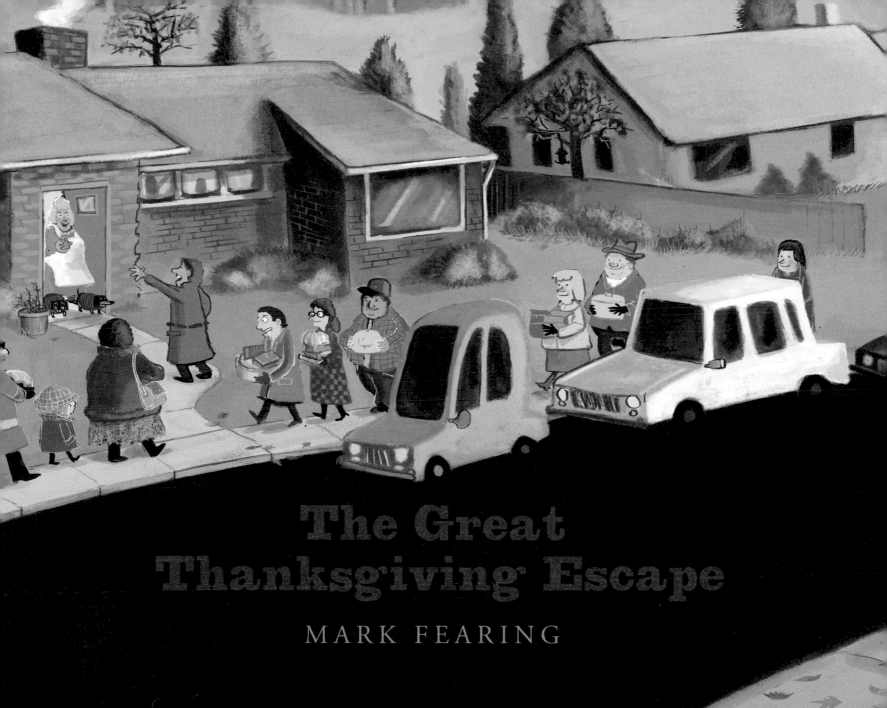

The Great Thanksgiving Escape

MARK FEARING

SCHOLASTIC INC.

It was another Thanksgiving at Grandma's.

"You can play in here with the rest of the kids," Gavin's mother told him. "We'll call you when the turkey's ready."

"Have fun!" Gavin's dad called.
But Gavin knew it was not going to be fun.
Not fun at all.

"Hey," someone whispered. It was his cousin Rhonda. "What do you say we break out of here and head for the swing set in the backyard?"

"I'm supposed to stay here until turkey time," Gavin said.

Rhonda climbed out from under the coats.

"The way I see it, Gav," she said, "is that sometimes you have to make your own fun."

"Are you with me?" she asked.

Gavin nodded. "I'm in."

They crept out and headed for the front door.

Suddenly, Rhonda jumped back.
"That way's blocked by vicious guard dogs.
I think they've picked up our scent!" she yelled.

"Run!"

But when they rounded the corner,
Rhonda stopped dead in her tracks.

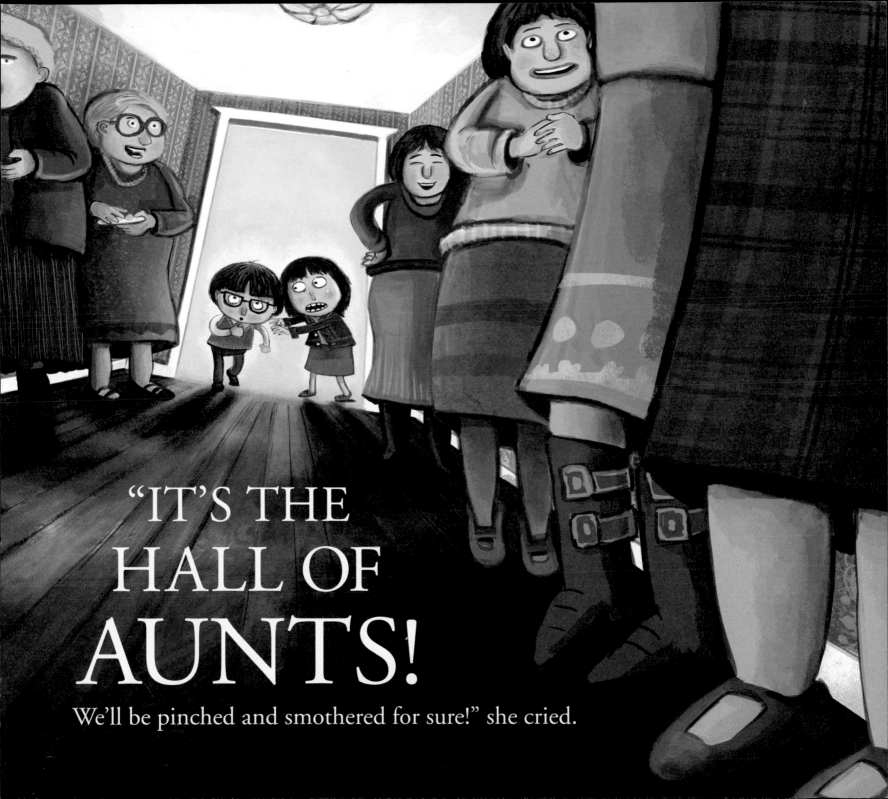

"IT'S THE HALL OF AUNTS!

We'll be pinched and smothered for sure!" she cried.

Gavin trembled, remembering Christmas last year.
He'd had to ice his face for three days.

They took off, but it was too late.
Rhonda had been grabbed.

Luckily she reacted defensively

AHHHHHH

and managed to break free
without a pinch.

CHOOOO

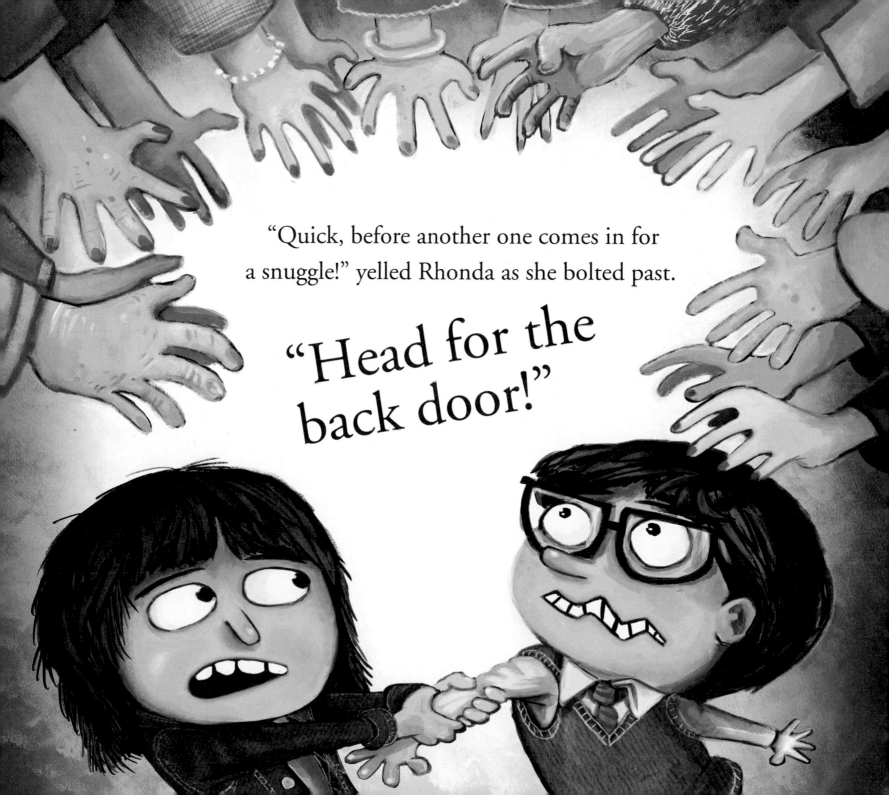

"Quick, before another one comes in for a snuggle!" yelled Rhonda as she bolted past.

"Head for the back door!"

"OH, NO—
THE GREAT
WALL OF
BUTTS!"

Rhonda yelled, "It's certain death
to get between them and the TV!"

"Down here," said Rhonda. "I bet there's
a way through the basement."

Gavin wasn't so sure. It looked dark and
smelled like dirty socks and hair gel.

They peeked cautiously around the corner.

"ZOMBIES!"

Rhonda screamed. "They'll eat our brains as an appetizer!"

They raced back up the stairs to the kitchen.
"Just a little snack for the road," Gavin said.
"No!" Rhonda yelled.

"It's a trap!"

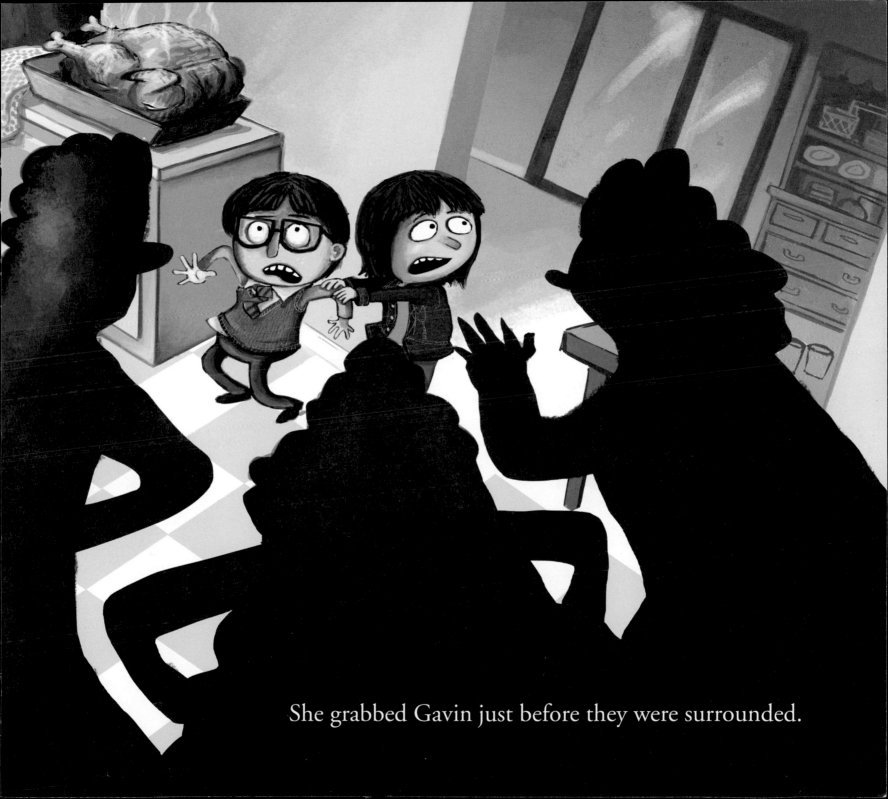

She grabbed Gavin just before they were surrounded.

They turned and sprinted for the door.

"We're almost there!"

But they skidded to a stop
when they reached the glass.

"At least we tried," Rhonda said.
Gavin was quiet for a moment.

Then he said, "The way I see it, Rhonda, is that sometimes you have to make your own fun."